THE BLUE MANGO COLLECTION

THE BLUE MANGO COLLECTION

FIVE SHORT STORIES

DARA GIRARD

ALSO BY DARA GIRARD

Collections

Domestic Disturbance (written as Dara Benton)

The Lady Next Door and Other Stories

Holiday Hearts

School Days: Five Story Collection

Lost and Found

Five Holiday Tales

10 Holiday Stories

When the Snow Falls

Henson Series

Table for Two

Gaining Interest

Careless Rapture

Dangerous Curves

Familiar Stranger

Clifton Sisters

The Sapphire Pendant

The Amber Stone

The Emerald Ring

Novels

Honest Betrayal

The Daughters of Winston Barnett

Remember My Name

Illusive Flame

Winterwood Lane

Piece of Cake

This Changes Everything

INTRODUCTION

In a city where many seek status and power, some humble souls seek connection and a taste of the Caribbean.

They'll find it in an unassuming DC restaurant founded by Drake Henson, a man with a painful past and a passion for food.

It's rumored that all sorts of people find their way to the Blue Mango restaurant and each has a story.

Here are a few of them...

In "An Extraordinary Request," a nervous new waitress faces a challenge when an elderly customer asks for an unusual dish.

"Cornered," follows a newly hired man who faces a critical decision that will affect his job and his future.

"The Scent of Memory," shows how a woman's hope of reconciliation with her ex-husband falters when the reason for their divorce walks in.

In "Left Unsaid," a couple's routine date night changes when a person's innocent remark forces them to face trouble in their marriage.

Finally in "Waiting on Yesterday," a woman's blind date goes from bad to worse when her 'date' finally shows up.

Welcome to the Blue Mango.

THE BLUE MANGO COLLECTION

AN EXTRAORDINARY REQUEST

AN EXTRAORDINARY REQUEST

"Oh no, he's back again."

"Who?" the new staffer asked, looking at her colleagues confused. The lunchtime rush at the Blue Mango had barely begun and yet the atmosphere in the DC restaurant was already grim, as if a stingy politician and his demanding mistress had walked through the doors. The four of them looked into the main dining hall, where the large windows welcomed the presence of a blazing June sun as two other employees welcomed patrons and began taking orders. A man waited by the doors to be seated. The new staffer didn't see anything particularly noticeable about him except that he was probably past seventy.

"Should I take it?" a waiter with a trim red beard and lips built to play the tuba asked. The new staffer kept forgetting his name.

"I usually do," the first waitress said with a sigh of

resignation. Her pressed black hair fell to her shoulders with elegant streaks of gold highlights. She usually wore a smile. It was missing today.

"I can give you a hand," Red Beard said.

"No, that's okay. I think I'll manage."

"Who is it?" the newer staffer added in a louder voice.

The three of them shared a look as startling as the sound of a loud gong in a tearoom and just as ominous, finally the most senior of the group, a slender woman with big ears who looked about thirty but had worked there the longest, said, "It's Mr. Reggie. He comes in once a month and asks for something that's not on the menu."

The new staffer furrowed her brows. "Why would he do that?"

Red Beard shrugged. "Nobody knows."

"And after he does that. He'll ask for something else not on the menu."

"Perhaps he's confused," the new staffer suggested, hoping to be helpful, but feeling ridiculous instead. Surely, they'd come to that conclusion on their own.

The three shared that look again—just as startling but not as ominous—then golden streaks shrugged and said, "Let her have a taste. It's a pretty interesting exchange."

The senior staff member frowned. "I don't think that's fair."

"Well, you'd better make a decision fast. The boss won't want us to keep anyone waiting."

The mood seemed to become grimmer as each of them imagined getting on the wrong side of the restaurant owner, Drake Henson.

"I don't mind," the new staffer said quickly, eager to prove herself. "I'm used to dealing with seniors."

"He's not your typical senior." Golden streaks handed her the menu. "You'll see," she said before the smile that had been missing suddenly returned.

It wasn't that Mr. Reggie looked harmless. He didn't. He sat tall and straight as if the back of his chair was a series of lightning rods. He'd removed his black felt hat, and it sat on the chair beside him as if it were expected company. He had thin lips and thick brows as white as cotton and a mustache to match.

"May I get you anything to drink?" Gina said as she watched him study the menu. The initial exchange didn't seem peculiar. She'd introduced herself and handed him the menu without incident.

"No, my dear," Mr. Reggie said, and she heard the trace of an accent that reminded her of a soft Caribbean breeze.

"Do you know what you'd like to order?"

He nodded. "Yes, I do." He closed the menu and

carefully set it on the table. "I'd like a bowl of peace and a side of anguish."

Gina stared at him for a moment, hoping her mouth hadn't fallen open. When her colleagues had told her he'd ask for something not on the menu she'd thought they'd meant food. Was he not quite the full wattage?

"Umm," she said, licking her lips and trying to choose her words wisely, "I'm afraid you can't eat peace or anguish."

Eyes the color of ginger tea met hers with studied patience as if he found her a bit simple. "Of course you can." He sighed. "But if you don't have that I'll have a taste of morning and a splash of afternoon."

This was ridiculous! She began to open her mouth to tell him that was impossible then paused. If he were a younger man, would she quickly dismiss him as dotty or senile? There was nothing in his voice or manner to suggest that. His words and manner were controlled. Was his request truly impossible? Was there a chance he was offering her a challenge? She looked at him and caught the hint of a smile, his sharp eyes bright with intelligence. She felt the brush of a connection she couldn't name, but she knew she wanted to figure it out. "Could you give me a moment?" she said.

He nodded.

She returned to the kitchen and approached Golden Streaks who'd just taken a plate to deliver. "I think it's a riddle."

"We don't do specialties here," the head chef frowned. "Tell him to go somewhere else."

"But—"

"I'm not entertaining strange—"

"What seems to be the problem?"

Gina turned and froze. Drake Henson, the owner of the restaurant, always scared her a little. She always wondered about the brave woman who'd taken on such a grim looking man as her spouse. Several workers said he wasn't all that scary, but to Gina, he reminded her of a lion with extracted claws ready to attack.

The chef's voice filled the kitchen with his disdain. "This newbie wants me to make a special dish for one of the weirdos."

"One of the what?"

"One of the weir—" The chef choked on the final word, suddenly realizing his mistake. Shamefaced, with all the bravado of a whipped puppy, he cleared his throat. "The patrons," he corrected.

Drake nodded. "Okay." He turned to Gina and pinned her with a look that made her wish she hadn't taken up Mr. Reggie's challenge. That she hadn't spoken up at all and had let Golden Streaks take his order. She'd only been working there a week and didn't want it to be her last. But the look on Mr. Henson's face made it a distinct possibility. "Explain."

She swallowed, suddenly doubting everything she'd considered. She saw him growing impatient and lost her nerve. "Never mind," she mumbled, then hurried out of the kitchen and regretfully told Mr. Reggie that she couldn't help him. He nodded with understanding, although he seemed disappointed.

She had a strange sense that he was more disappointed in her than not getting his strange request, but she pushed the thought aside. She tried to interest him in a dessert, but he shook his head, took his hat off the chair, and left.

SHE HAD a wretched night wishing she'd tried harder, twisting on the stiff twin bed, pounding a pillow that refused to soften. Not that a sleepless night was anything new. She'd gotten used to the low shimmering anxiety that sat heavily on her chest ever since she'd lost her last job at a furniture retail chain that had gone bankrupt. Her roommates seemed to have their lives together—one was already a successful real estate agent, the other a math teacher at a prestigious high school. She feared she wouldn't be of any help to the man, to anyone. At twenty-seven, she felt as if she were floundering in life. But Mr. Reggie's request gave her a renewed purpose.

She wondered if she had been on to something. Had the old man been speaking in riddles? Or had she made it up and was it pure nonsense? What food was like peace? What flavor was like morning and a taste of afternoon?

The next day, she asked one of her colleagues about him.

"None of us know much. I think I overheard that he was a Windrush kid."

Windrush? She'd heard that name before, vaguely mentioned by a grandfather and possibly an auntie, but she hadn't paid much attention. Hearing about some grand ship that took people from the Caribbean to England held little interest to her at the time.

Now it did.

She typed in the word Windrush on her laptop. The ship, named HMT Empire Windrush, which would give a generation of people their unifying distinction, was one of the many documents that came up during her search.

On the screen appeared a picture dated 1948 featuring sharply dressed young black men seeking post-war work in England. She saw the face of strangers and yet their ambitions and hope stretched out to her across the years. It was a hope that hadn't wavered with time: A dream of a better life.

She knew the men in the photo were the fortunate ones able to pay the fee to arrive on British shores while those without means would not be able to leave countries with a lack of work, or lack of opportunities. A number of the men were likely familiar with England because they were ex-servicemen, although their loyalty to the crown was not always acknowledged.

Mr. Reggie was too young to be from the first wave that came. Although the wave continued until 1971, and Gina read through many documents, she still couldn't make a connection and wondered why she had tried.

This wasn't England, after all. And while the Blue Mango served Caribbean food it didn't warrant such an odd request. What could he be referring to? Why was she so certain he was referring to anything?

She had to ask someone who may be able to help.

Auntie Shirleen's house always smelled like sunshine and chocolate biscuits.

Gina sat in the sitting room, trying not to catch the frozen gaze of the numerous framed pictures of friends and family lining the room. She balanced a fine china teacup in her lap, wishing her aunt didn't have the habit of being so formal, while her aunt settled a white plate of biscuits on the coffee table.

She made her chocolate chip cookies with bread flour (instead of all-purpose) and they always came out crispy on the edges and sinfully sweet and chewy, Gina remembered that her mother always made her cookies out of all-purpose flour because they didn't have the money for bread flour and Gina had felt a little cheated when she'd gone to her cousin's house and tasted how cookies were supposed to be made.

She remembered her father chiding her, saying her tongue shouldn't be richer than her wallet.

At fifty-seven, Auntie Shirleen had long grey hair she'd pulled back into one braid and a body of soft curves that hinted at her love of food, but her words were always sharp, although her British accent at times managed to soften the blow. However, this time it didn't.

"What do you want?" she said.

"I'm not sure."

Auntie Shirleen laughed. "That's nice to hear. So few people say that anymore. People are so certain of the wrong things." She took a sip of tea. "You look like you have questions."

She did. But now she didn't know where to start. Did she tell her about the customer? Did she ask her about the Windrush ship?

"What do you want to know?"

"If someone were to ask you for...say a bowl of peace, what would you serve them?"

Auntie Shirleen leaned back, and her gaze sharpened. "Why?"

Gina shrugged, trying to appear nonchalant, but her aunt wasn't fooled. She asked, "What would *you* serve?"

"I don't know. That's why I'm here."

Her aunt closed her eyes. "I remember my first sight of snow..."

Gina felt herself growing impatient. She'd heard

the story before, but her aunt said the tale as if it were the first time and not the hundredth. Then she talked about her first taste of mushy peas, the feel of damp in their first London flat. How it seemed to hover in the air and press on their skin as if it could flatten them into the ground.

She looked at the soft glow on her aunt's brown face and then truly began to listen as if her aunt was becoming fully formed in front of her and not some made-up compilation of a person. But an actual person. She'd never taken a moment to imagine what these experiences had truly felt like.

She'd never been eager to hear what her aunt had to say. Never found her interesting enough.

But for the first time, she listened. Like she hadn't done before. She wanted to hear what she had to say. This woman, who always seemed to live in the vast foreign land of memory. Who would at times pull her aside and tell her how she still struggled with the metric system.

Perhaps...it wasn't about memory. But something else.

Gina bit into a cookie. She remembered how her mother's were more brittle, not as succulent, but she hadn't noticed that at first. She remembered the scent of the cookies filling up the house, and the joy on her mother's face as she placed the cookies on a plate. The sight of her brother's chubby hand as he snuck one, her father's laughter as he teased his wife about spoiling them. The cookies had tasted like heaven. There had been nothing to compare them to. Nothing to steal away the moment and make her want them to be different.

She never ate her mother's cookies with the same joy again once she'd tasted something better.

But she realized it wasn't only because of the lack of expensive flour. In her own bitter ungratefulness, she'd missed the savory taste of care and love mixed into the batter.

That shamed her.

As she left Auntie Shirleen's house under a June evening sky littered with stars, she thought of all the stories she'd missed, the flavors she'd forgotten. The senses she'd let die.

It had taken a lot of courage to go to Mr. Henson's office but because it was his business, he was the only one who could request a special order from the chef. She remembered trying not to wring her hands as she walked down the hall, wondering how she should share her idea for a special meal that could use items already on the premises.

She'd cleared her throat before she knocked on the door and carefully opened it when he sternly said, "Come."

She halted in the doorway when she saw he wasn't

alone. A full-figured, brown-skinned woman was holding up his trashbin. She wore a black and white exercise outfit, which gave her the appearance of a cuddly panda bear.

"Oh, I'll come back," Gina said.

"No," he said, "it's fine."

"But I don't think it's something to discuss in front of the cleaning crew."

His eyes turned onyx, and he shot out of his seat so fast that Gina let out a tiny scream.

"It's okay, Drake," the panda bear woman said in a gentle voice.

"No, it's not." He shifted his lethal gaze back to her. "She happens to be my wife."

Gina felt like jumping out the window and running down the street, possibly to get mercifully crushed by machinery. She wanted to die and Drake Henson seemed willing to oblige her—using his bare hands. She shifted to the woman, trying not to show the shock on her face. She was an attractive woman but she hadn't imagined her boss with a woman like her.

Mrs. Henson seemed to sense her horror and laughed. "It's okay. It's an honest mistake."

No, it wasn't. It was devastating. She wouldn't be surprised if he fired her on the spot.

"What did you want?" someone asked her. She wasn't quite sure who since her heart pounded so loud in her ears, she could hardly process anything else.

She took a step back, shaking her head. "I don't think—"

"Sit down," this command came from Drake. She'd noticed his mouth move while his wife's remained closed. Her legs obeyed before her mind could catch up.

"My name's Cassie," his wife said. "What's your name?"

"Gina," she managed to say, her voice barely above a whisper.

"Is this about Mr. Reggie?" Cassie said.

She stared at her, stunned.

"Drake told me you were interested in him."

Somehow, she hadn't thought him sharing that information but perhaps there was more to him than scary dark eyes and a frown.

"Stop glaring at her," his wife said.

"I'm not glaring." He clasped his hands together, his gaze never leaving Gina's face. "I'm listening."

Gina cleared her throat. "Once a month he comes in and requests things not on the menu, like 'peace in a bowl' or something."

Cassie spoke up, "Maybe it is on the menu."

Gina frowned and said, "What?" at the same time, Drake said, "Go on."

Mrs. Henson licked her lip, thoughtful. "What if it's a way to connect? Who's to say that those things aren't on the menu? Sometimes it's not about what's in front of us but rather what we're willing to see. When the world deems you invisible, sometimes you have to come up with other ways to be seen. To connect."

Drake looked at his wife and Gina saw a brief, unguarded look of such love and respect. She was a little jealous and fell a little in love with Cassie herself. She saw an amazing woman with a keen insight.

It made sense. What if he wasn't asking for something special, but a way to connect? She hadn't considered that. She'd thought he was trying to recapture a memory or a forgotten flavor. Perhaps all he wanted was to be seen.

"Thank you," Gina said, jumping out of her seat. "I now know what I can do."

SHE WAITED for him to return the next month.

And he did. He brought with him the scent of the Potomac River mingled with the scent of fireworks.

She made sure to be the one to find him a seat and hand him a menu. She felt possessive of this particular patron who confounded her.

"What would you like to drink?"

"Nothing, dear." He said with a twinkle in his eye.

"Do you know what you want to eat?"

"A bowl of peace and a side of anguish."

"We don't have that. How about something else?"

"A taste of morning and a little afternoon."

She nodded. "I'll see what I can do.

She returned to the table carrying a plate with yellow rice, curried zucchini, and sliced spicy chicken. "We were all out of morning with a touch of afternoon, but I hope a touch of evening works instead?"

His eyes lit up. "Yes, yes indeed." He said and smiled.

And she smiled too realizing that he'd also served her a wonderful meal. A meal—one filled with the delectable flavor of peace mingled with the refreshing aroma of possibility—that nourished her soul. He reminded her that life wasn't a series of tests, that there were times one made up the answer to questions.

That making up the answer was what life was all about. Not knowing the answer. Many times, there were many answers to one question.

He reminded her that life wasn't only about grand gestures or big adventures, about the haunting past or distant futures, but tiny moments of connection where one person says to another: I see you. Wanna play?

And the other says: Yes.

CORNERED

CORNERED

He'd already lost ten pounds.

After leaving his last job because of stomach cramps, muscle spasms, and a nervous tick he still hadn't been able to shake, the last thing he needed was dinner with his department head—a man built with the sturdy physique of a red brick schoolhouse, that could withstand both a hurricane and typhoon—and the six other colleagues, the Demon Lord...uh head, had invited.

Dayton had only been in the work world for five years and had already switched jobs three times. The first company had phased out his position. The second hadn't been the right match. But the third had been less than charming (soul-crushing was how he usually remembered it in his nightmares). He'd ended up with a boss who took keen pleasure in humiliating him every chance he could get. Belittled his every action, shouted, and threw things and no one seemed to care because this boss brought in a lot of clients and money for the company. Dayton knew he had to leave. Anything had to be better than this.

He was certain of it.

Now he wasn't so sure.

He left the raucous sound of the city behind, and its cool breath of autumn, as he crossed the threshold of the Blue Mango restaurant and, for a brief, tender moment he let his gaze settle on a plate of halibut on a bed of yellow rice, the spicy scent of black pepper biting his nose.

He bit the inside of his cheek, imagining the succulent taste of the dish.

He knew exactly what he'd order.

But before he could congratulate himself on his selection, his gaze shifted, and he had to grit his teeth to stop himself from doubling over in pain.

His stomach cramped as if gripped in a fiery vise, slowly cranking tighter and tighter. He stared at the sight of the long table crowded with office workers and he feared he wouldn't be able to eat a thing (or if he did, how long he'd manage to keep it down).

He silently swore. How had this happened? He was certain he'd gotten the time right for the celebratory dinner. One of their team had gotten a promotion and was leaving for a different division. Dayton had planned to arrive early enough to make his way to the table and grab a chair unnoticed, but there was only one seat left.

One dreadful seat.

He took a hasty step back. Perhaps he could leave without anyone...

A colleague noticed him and waved him over with a bright smile of greeting. Dayton barely had the strength to wave back. He'd taken some stomach medicine so that he could at least pretend to smile without pain, perhaps even drink something, but the effect hadn't kicked in yet.

He feared he wouldn't even be able to make it over to the table without shuffling like a zombie. He took a deep breath and plastered on a smile, sweat gathering on his forehead, each step towards the table a little more agonizing than the last.

But he could do this.

He had to.

Perhaps it had all been in his head. Maybe it wouldn't be so bad. What were the chances of going from one abusive supervisor to another? His odds had to be improving, right?

Heart pounding, throat dry, Dayton carefully lowered himself onto the dreaded wooden chair, determined to make it through the evening.

When they'd placed their orders, he allowed himself to relax a little. Perhaps it won't be so bad...

He felt the hand on his thigh. The warm, solid

pressure. He swallowed. He could ignore it. He'd done it in the past.

The first time he'd felt the hand had been a shock.

Two weeks into his new job, he'd taken a ride in the elevator and then, as he stepped out, he felt something brush against his behind. He turned, sure that it had to be his imagination. The somber-looking man with the too-thin tie, the one who'd been introduced as his supervisor, wouldn't have just touched him, would he?

Weeks passed, and Dayton soon became certain that he'd imagined it. It was nothing. Just his nerves. Perhaps, innocently, a bag or notebook had touched him. Sure, the elevator hadn't been that crowded, but Dayton had walked around him to exit the elevator. It was probably his fault. He could be clumsy.

Then came the day in the break room.

His boss had thrown out a comment about how Dayton's suit fit him well. Flustered by the compliment, strangely flattered and disturbed, Dayton had just mumbled 'Thanks,' ready to dismiss it until his boss whispered, "I bet you'd look just as good out of it."

He didn't know how to respond, and his supervisor seemed to know this because he just grinned in a manner that made Dayton's pulse race like a trapped animal. He'd hurried out of the room, forgetting his freshly made coffee on the counter.

He sat at his desk, his mind racing, feeling foolish,

cowardly, and scared. Had he overreacted? Should he have brushed it aside? Laughed? Ignored it?

He rubbed his sweaty hands on his lap, trying to regain control of his pounding heart. He didn't know what to do or say. Did he go to Human Resources? Would anyone at HR believe him? He wasn't that good looking nor was he a standout employee. People might think he was trying to get attention.

This situation was like his old job but worse. At least there the actions were visible. The throwing of objects, the shouting, but this time the assaults (was that even the right word?) were soft, subtle, personal. They felt like they were aimed only at him. Meant just for him. Only him. That he'd been targeted.

But maybe if he stayed away, became more assertive, that could change things.

He was too nice. His friends always said so. His family too. He was a target because he acted like one. If he presented himself with more bravado...

He never wore that suit again, even though it had been a favorite, and started working out at his apartment gym, working on his posture, working on his voice, working on himself. There had to be something wrong with him, so he'd fix it and then everything would be okay.

And it worked.

No unwanted attention, no side comments, no unexpected touches. For two weeks. He'd won. It didn't hurt that his boss was gone for a week to a convention.

Then he returned and Dayton hadn't known it until he'd stood up from his desk and felt a hand cup his butt. He turned sharply, too stunned to speak. By now his boss was far enough away to make it appear as if it hadn't happened. Dayton briefly caught the gaze of two colleagues as if to say, *Did you see that?* but they quickly glanced away. No one looked at him. Or rather, they openly avoided doing so. It wasn't their business. It wasn't their problem. It was his. His alone.

A couple of weeks of nothing and then...this dinner.

And the hand on his thigh made it clear his boss wasn't afraid to exert his power.

He knew Dayton needed this job. His parents were so glad he wore a suit and tie instead of overalls like generations before him.

He didn't mind being an office worker. Choosing a different path had made him feel like an adult, forging his own destiny. But so far, the world of work had been a series of egos and power trips, something he'd never been adept at handling.

He thought of the advice he'd been given from well-meaning family and friends.

"Don't say anything. It'll probably stop. You don't want to cause trouble."

"Take it as a compliment."

"Probably a phase that'll end."

"Perhaps you'll get promoted if you handle it right."

None of the advice made Dayton feel better. They made him feel petty and small. No one seemed to be outraged. Most found it amusing, and some found it cute. He felt belittled all over again, as if he was making a big deal out of nothing. Some questioned his interpretation of the situation as if they were trying to be fair and judge both sides, and the side they seemed to choose was the one with the power.

And he was powerless.

Dayton moved his leg away and reached for his water glass just to keep his body in motion.He looked up and nearly choked. He was pinned by a gaze that he'd avoided before. An older colleague, known for his shoulder-length locs and expensive suits, who never smiled, never chatted but had a fierce reputation. Dayton envied him and feared him a little. Did he see his weakness? Did he despise him as much as he despised himself?

DAYTON ESCAPED TO THE RESTROOM, hiding in one of the stalls, feeling very much the coward he imagined everyone thought he was. After a few seconds, he heard water rushing and decided to leave. He took a deep breath, opened the stall door, then froze.

For a panicked moment, he thought the man at the

sink was his boss, the sound of water splashing into the basin mingling with the thudding of his heart. They were alone. There was no one else in the bathroom.

The sound of water abruptly stopped as the man turned off the faucet, descending the room into silence.

It wasn't his boss.

It was the other man.

The older colleague, the who frightened him for entirely different reasons.

The one who made him feel ashamed. Weak.

Their eyes met in the mirror. The older man's dark gaze pinned Dayton with the power of a shadow creature that could penetrate his soul. Dayton stayed mute and could only stare.

"This is how it works," the older man said in a bored tone, pulling a paper towel from the dispenser and casually drying his hands. "He's not going anywhere. He's going to rule here until this organization gets tired of him. He's going to make your life miserable, and you need to decide how much BS you're willing to swallow." He tossed the paper away and folded his hands. "You can complain but it won't help. You can try to confront him but that won't help either. This is a rotten company and a bright young thing like you won't change it. But you can learn from it. Learn that you deserve better and get out. If you stay, you'll be rewarded for the amount of BS you're willing to swallow."

Dayton opened his mouth but the older man held up his hand and Dayton closed his mouth again.

"One day," the man continued. "Maybe in a couple of months if you're lucky, or years from now if you're not, you'll look at yourself in the mirror and you won't even recognize what a real smile looks like anymore. You would have compromised, forced your lips into a contortion of emotions you've never really felt. You won't know what genuine feelings are anymore. But you'll justify your actions to yourself because that's all you'll have left. Dignity, self-worth, integrity you would have given them all up.

"You always have a choice. They'll make you believe that you don't. That only losers quit, that if you're strong you'll stick it out, but sooner or later you'll see that it's the losers who stay, the ones who suck it up and keep their heads down, those who let people climb on their backs with the hopes they'll be lifted up someday. It may happen. But it may not happen to you. It's a gamble. But it's not a gamble you have to take.

"You have no power over him, but you are not powerless."

Dayton swallowed hard. Why did his words sound like a trick, a test, a riddle? He was one of the longest employees. Did he see him as a threat? "Why are you still here?" Dayton managed to ask.

The man shook his head with a shade of regret, the overhead lights catching glints of silver in the dark locs.

"Can't you recognize a coward when you see one? I got the same lecture years ago but stayed too long and now I have too much to lose. The world is bigger than this place. Get out and see it."

Dayton heard the words—felt the warning—but wondered why he was afraid to believe them, to really believe that he had a choice, that he could be rid of this feeling of failure, inadequacy, hopelessness. It had been so long since he hadn't felt that way. When had it become his default?

Dayton closed his eyes, listened to the sound of shoes heading for the door, the slight squeak of a door opening then softly swinging shut.

He opened his eyes.

What did he do now? Did he follow him? Did he return back to the table and then formally quit later? Did he pretend the conversation never happened?

He started to return to his seat, then his stomach started to ache again, a warning of danger.

He walked past the table and outside into the fresh air, a new feeling seizing him. Panic. What had he done? It wasn't too late to turn around and go back.

But he didn't move. People hustled past him, going in different directions.

He didn't know which direction to go, but he started walking. And kept walking until his stomach didn't hurt anymore.

~

DAYTON WALKED several blocks not knowing that he'd return to the Blue Mango nearly six months later able to eat the spicy halibut on a bed of yellow rice, able to laugh with his new colleagues at a different company, able to look at himself in the mirror with pride.

The new position wasn't impressive, but the job was interesting and in a field he cared about. He wouldn't have found it if he'd stayed where he was.

If he hadn't taken that first step.

If he hadn't realized he always had a choice.

That a choice wasn't always easy.

But it was always his to make.

THE SCENT OF MEMORY

THE SCENT OF MEMORY

IT WAS A THING. Having a divorce anniversary. Minah Tate heard a friend had done it and thought that after two years it was time for her to try it too. Not that she'd make it a ritual but it'd be nice to try once.

She walked into the Blue Mango and the buoyant din of voices made the restaurant seem more crowded than it actually was. However, there were few empty tables and wait staff efficiently made their way to patrons, one waitress passing by Minah carrying a dish spiced with curry that made her stomach growl. One such table seated a middle-aged man with brown skin and a silver goatee, which didn't match his black hair. Although his gaze was lowered, she knew he had kind brown eyes and an easy laugh.

Her ex-husband was early as usual. Or perhaps she was late. When he looked up from his menu she waved. He smiled.

"Have you ordered?" Minah asked taking the seat across from him.

"No," he said, casting a glance over her in a way that gave her a slight thrill. She was glad she'd chosen the business casual satin blouse and skirt to match his dark trousers and maroon sweater. Neither were over-dressed or underdressed. "I was waiting for you."

She lifted up the menu. "You know what I like."

"Your tastes might have changed."

"Few things about me have changed except—" She stopped and bit her lip.

Perhaps this divorce anniversary hadn't been such a good idea. Because that was the problem. She hadn't changed. Not enough. She still liked him. Loved him even, if she were being completely honest. He was one of the few people whose company she enjoyed. She found he was very easy to like. She still held a faint glimmer of hope that things could return to how they used to be.

But she brushed the thought aside determined to enjoy the evening.

Yellow rice and jerk chicken.

They ordered and she'd expected the conversation to be stilted but it was as if no time had passed. He still remembered that she worked at a nonprofit and asked about the funding, they'd been together for five years total, married three. She still couldn't believe how it had ended, how she'd never seen it coming, although others had warned her.

And she didn't want to think about what happened until *she* walked into the restaurant.

Stylish, five foot seven, and full of attitude and she hated Minah's guts. Simon's daughter, from his first marriage, hadn't seemed much of a problem at the beginning of their budding relationship. Until she had problems at the university, at the dorms, at work, with her mother. She was always blameless and her father was blind to any of her flaws.

Even her mother felt sorry for Minah. "I know we spoiled her," she once said with regret at the wedding for their son. "Perhaps you'll be a good influence." She said the words as if she thought that Minah could be the remedy. She couldn't. She became enemy number one.

She undermined her and insulted her. It was war and her ex managed to disappear until the battle ended —usually with his daughter in tears.

Minah eventually confronted her husband. She said they had to make changes.

Clearly, the changes had meant only her.

She shouldn't have married him. She didn't realize that divorce could be so expensive especially when he listened to his daughter about the house, about what to split.

Minah wondered if he loved her at all. He said he

did but that Julie was his blood. His life. He begged for her to understand and she tried but felt her resentment building.

This daughter was ruining a perfect relationship.

Except it wasn't perfect. She realized that something so easily broken hadn't been that solid.

But she still wondered if there could be a chance.

And that feeling grew as time passed and it felt as if they'd never been apart.

Then she looked up and nearly lost her dinner.

SHE WAS THERE.

Julie slithered over to the table, a ready smile in place. "Dad? I thought it was you."

He beamed. "Hello, love. Fancy seeing you here."

"Mind if I sit down," she said not caring what the answer would be as she pulled out a chair and staked claim. "Hello, Minah."

Minah nodded. She was still trying to keep her dinner down. She looked across the table at lovely brown eyes as dead as a graveyard.

Minah waited for Simon to say something. To let his daughter know that it wasn't okay for her to eat with them. That this was just to be them for just one night.

"It's great to see you," he said, "but this dinner is really a private one."

Yes, at last. He'd learned to stand up to her. Minah felt her heart lift until she saw the woman's lip twitch.

"I'm so sorry. How rude it's just..." She sighed as if the world were coming to an end. Her voice trembled slightly when she spoke. "My boss shouted at me today and it was so humiliating."

Minah's heart sank as she watched Simon's kind brown eyes soften in compassion. She watched him fall for the show as he always did. Any time he tried to set boundaries Julie had a drama to share. And in her stories, she always played the villain—uh—victim: Friends who were mean, boyfriends who were jerks, colleagues who were spiteful, baristas who ignored her.

"And I was going to meet with friends but they bailed on me."

Simon shifted his soft gaze to Minah with a silent plea. She'd grown so used to it. It was the look that helped her decide to divorce him. The look that said, 'she needs me' 'just this once' 'come on have some compassion.'

The only role Julie wanted to cast her in was villain or forgettable stock character. She wasn't in the mood to play either, so she met his gaze and Minah shrugged.

The gesture seemed to appease him because a soft smile of gratitude touched his lips and he looked at her as if perhaps she did have a chance.

But the witch also sent her a look.

A look of triumph.

A look that said she'd won.

MINAH WENT TO THE LADIES' room. She wasn't sick, thankfully, but she couldn't taste anything anymore. Her memory had betrayed her. She'd forgotten how bad it truly had been being with Simon. How much pain she'd endured and how he'd been the one to leave. How she'd foolishly believed he'd one day realize his mistake and come back to her. She should be the first to leave this time.

She turned and saw a teenager who hadn't seemed to grow into her body or looks yet. She stood like a gangly flamingo in a dress she'd outgrown. Minah tried not to stare as a braided hair piece began to unravel at the back. The teenager looked distraught as she washed her hands.

Or rather over-washed them. She'd wash, then dry them, then wash them again.

Minah cleared her throat. "Is...are you okay?"

The teenager turned to her. She had tiny brown eyes and a pointed chin that made her face look harsh, but her reply was anything but, it was soft and unsure. "I'm supposed to say I'm fine, right?"

Minah wasn't sure how to respond.

"My mother says that people ask but they're not really interested so I shouldn't burden them with the truth. It's not polite."

"So, what's the problem?"

She blinked.

"That's a question you can answer without worrying about politeness and niceties, right?"

The teenager rewarded her with a smile. "I guess so."

Minah took a hesitant step forward. "First, do you mind if I uh...fix your hair?"

"No, not that it'll make a difference."

Minah took hold of the wayward braid and began to pin it in place. "It will. You look nice."

"She doesn't think so."

"She?"

"My dad's fiancée. She can't stand me and my dad doesn't see it."

Minah paused. How could their situations sound so similar?

"Dad wanted us to have this dinner so that we can, I don't know, bond or something. But it's not working. She makes fun of what I wear, what I eat, what I do. He said I should be thankful that she's interested. I love my dad but sometimes he can be so –"

"Dense, clueless, naïve?"

She smiled. "Yeah." She tilted her head. "Is your dad like that?"

Minah briefly thought of her father who'd been distraught by her divorce and had wondered if she'd worked hard enough to keep it together. 'Marriage takes compromise,' he used to tell her. 'It was no bed of roses between your mother and me but we made it work.'

She'd tried, but she hadn't made it to the forty-year mark like her parents. She'd barely made it to seven.

"No," Minah said with a sigh, "but someone else I care about is." She hesitated. "Have you told your mother how you feel?"

"She's no longer with us."

"I'm sorry."

"Me too." The teenager sighed and rolled her eyes. "Guess who wants to be my 'new' mother. I mean, what the hell is that about? It's gross. I don't need a new mother." She sent her a look and quickly added, "And it's not like I want my dad to be lonely, I wish... it's just I wish..." She fell silent.

"It wasn't her," Minah finished for her.

She nodded.

It felt strange to see two different futures. Minah had hoped for a reconciliation that she knew wouldn't happen. And this young woman saw a future under the thumb of a woman who didn't like her.

"It won't last forever," she said. "One day you'll move out."

"And he wouldn't even miss me."

"I'm sure that's not true."

The teenager sent Minah a glance. And Minah understood, it was possible. She didn't think her ex had any regrets about the end of their marriage. No matter how much it hurt, he didn't miss her. Never would.

Julie might one day give him grandkids or might not. She might stay in town or move away and only see him infrequently. He might end up alone never realizing that his daughter had scared away any potential companionship.

And he might be just fine. He wasn't someone she had to worry about anymore.

This young woman's father may be blind to the pain he was causing her. She'd have to accept that.

A thought struck her. "You know what?" Minah said, feeling her mood brighten. "I think we should give your father and my ex exactly what they want."

"Your ex?"

"Yes, we were having a great divorce anniversary dinner until his daughter, who would probably happily see me beheaded, showed up and joined us."

"And he didn't say anything."

"No."

The teenager chewed her lip. "So how do we give them what they want?"

"Have you eaten yet?"

"Only the appetizer."

"Same here. What if I get us a table and we eat together?"

The teenager looked hopeful then her face fell. "My father would never allow that. He'd say it's bad manners and that the only reason we're here is to bond as a family."

"You could say you'll have plenty of time to bond later."

She shook her head. "No, he can be very stubborn."

"What do you think he'd do if you invited me to eat with you?"

"I don't know."

"Then let's find out."

"But what about your ex?"

"I'd rather eat with a stranger than have to suffer another second with a woman who made three years of my life a misery." Minah turned to the mirror and checked her lipstick. "Go back to your table and I'll join you shortly."

The teenager stared at her as if she didn't believe her.

"I promise." When the teenager still didn't move, she said, "What's your name?"

"Andrea."

"I'm Minah and I'll see you in a couple minutes. We're going to take back this evening."

WHEN MINAH RETURNED to the table Simon had the grace to look worried. "I was about to get Julie to check in on you," he said.

"Why? So, she can shove my head in the toilet?"

He frowned. "That's not funny."

"No, it's not."

"Sit down," he said and then, "Why aren't you sitting down?"

"Because we both know this night is over." She kissed him on the cheek. "I'll always love you." She looked over at Julie who looked surprised. Like a predator whose prey had managed to escape.

He stood alarmed. "Maybe we could—"

"No, never." And she knew that now even if he didn't. She turned and searched the restaurant until she spotted Andrea.

She went to the table. "Andrea! Imagine seeing you here." She sat down.

"Excuse me this is—"

"I'll tell you what this is," Minah said gesturing to the three of them, "This is a lie. You're making your daughter miserable and you don't care. It's not your fault because you're in love and you think she's a typical teenager, whatever that is, moody, rude, and reticent. But the truth is she doesn't like your fiancée and your fiancée doesn't like her. You love them both so you're going to keep them both and that's that. Own it. But don't force them to be friends because they won't be."

Andrea's father shook his head. "I'm not going to be lectured to by some stranger."

"Fine. I'm going to take your daughter and sit over there." She pointed to a distant table. "Come on."

She stood.

"Sit down," her father ordered.

"Why?" Andrea said in a sad voice. "So we can look like a family even though we don't feel like one? I want you to be happy and she makes you happy and that's all I have to say."

He grabbed his daughter's arm, stopping her. "Adjustments take time. You're not giving her a chance. You're being selfish."

"Sir—"

He glared at Minah and raised his voice. "Stay away from my family. This is none of your business."

A waiter rushed over. "I'm sorry, but you'll have to lower your voice or leave."

"Yes," Minah said, "shouting won't make your words clearer. You can't shame me into anything. You're really angry at yourself that a stranger had to show you what you didn't want to see. You're the selfish one. She'd old enough to make her decisions. She's humoring you. We are now going to sit at another table."

Andrea met her father's gaze. He let her arm go. "It's not like that."

"I know you don't think so," she said in a sad voice, "but it is."

~

"I'm shaking," Andrea said sitting at a table Minah had managed to get for them. "I never told him how I felt before."

"Do you regret it?"

"A little."

"Why?"

She shrugged. "I don't know. I thought it might change him, you know? I thought he might, I don't know, push the wedding back or something?"

"Or not marry her at all?"

Andrea flashed an embarrassed grin. "Yeah. I guess I really saw how much he prefers to be with her than with me and it hurts."

"I know."

"Is he looking over here?"

Minah stole a glance then shook her head.

"I probably shouldn't have asked that. I already knew the answer, but I guess I wanted to be wrong. I wanted to think that somehow, I'd ruined his evening. That he'd miss me, that he'd say he was sorry. But he never does."

Minah saw the girl's misery and didn't quite know what to say, although she knew exactly how she felt. She too had foolishly hoped that Simon would have stopped her, that she would have grasped even a minor victory over Julie but then she realized she was focusing on the wrong thing.

These two people who they cared about would never be who they wanted them to be, or in Andrea's case, needed them to be. He wouldn't be the kind of father who would look out for her, who would put her needs above his own, he was a vain, selfish man and was marrying his match. She would have to endure that until she was old enough to leave. But she didn't have to endure alone.

"I wish I had a daughter like you. Your father is missing out on a lot but it's his loss, not yours. Tonight, we're going to enjoy ourselves because we deserve it. It doesn't matter if they don't notice us. I notice you and you notice me and that's more than most people get."

At first, they pretended to forget, they pretended not to notice they weren't being noticed but as the time passed, as they bathed in the warmth of each other's smile, took solace in their true genuine interest and connection with each other. They didn't have to pretend.

That night they didn't know they'd formed a bond that would last them through many ups and downs. A friendship that would last more than many marriages, filled with a love they could both depend on.

One thing Minah knew as she left the Blue Mango that night was that joy was always ahead if you were bold enough to seize it.

Nearly a half hour later she was halfway up the

steps to her apartment building when she heard the wailing of a child.

"Shh, shh it's going to be okay."

She turned towards the sidewalk and the darkness of the gentle evening only allowed her to see the shadow of a man kneeling in front of a child whose loud screeches deafened the sound of traffic passing by.

She hurried over to them and as she got closer, she saw that the child, a girl whose two braids had become slightly askew and whose red skirt had been torn, sat on the ground cradling her bruised and bloodied knee.

"What happened?" she asked.

"A bicycle rider jumped up on the pavement and startled her. As she tried to get out of the way she fell on her knee. She gets nervous when she's in the city."

"You poor thing," Minah said to the child who looked to be about five or six. "Let's get this cleaned up. My apartment's right here and I live on the second floor. It won't take long."

"I wouldn't want to—"

She stood. "It's okay. I don't mind. Not only can we clean the wound but I also have ointment and plenty of bandages. Come on."

The child's cry turned to hiccups, then sniffles. Finally, once Minah cleaned the wound and put a bandage on the wound, the child fell silent.

The child took her hand. Minah gently squeezed it and smiled.

"Thanks," a deep voice said.

Minah turned sharply to the source, having forgotten anyone else was there (he'd been so quiet throughout the ordeal) then gasped. She'd focused so much attention on the child she hadn't noticed the man. If she had she might not have so casually invited him into her apartment.

When he wasn't cradling his daughter he seemed like a different man, on the hard side of thirty-eight with specks of grey.

If anyone looked like they could fell an oak tree with their bare hands, he did. He loomed large with folded arms, thin lips, and hard eyes that looked far from kind. If she'd seen that face, she wouldn't have dared touch his daughter. If she got an infection, would he sue? He knew where she lived.

He opened his jacket and pulled out his wallet. She held her breath, half expecting him to pull out his identification as a detective and tell her she was under arrest.

He pulled out a business card. "If you ever need a favor let me know."

She read the name Dennis Widby, data analysis/risk management. What? No way did he look like someone who sat behind a computer and assessed data points.

She nodded and pulled out her own card. "And if you ever need help looking more like a nerd let me know."

He laughed. His laughter surprised her. "People are always surprised by what I do."

"You have to admit you don't fit the profile."

"Part of it's on purpose."

"And the other part?"

He paused then said with a devious grin. "Perhaps it's *all* on purpose. Otherwise, I'm average."

He was anything but that. But he seemed less fierce now. Perhaps his eyes weren't hard, just worried. He'd been frazzled by his daughter's accident after all. He wasn't bad looking...

No...not doing that again. Not getting my heart broken. What was with her being attracted to men with kids? Who was to say he was a single dad anyway?

"It's a new career choice for me. I've been making a lot of changes recently including moving here from Ohio. It hasn't been easy since my wife's passing."

Really? Did he have to say that? What are the odds?

"You're doing great," Minah said eager to see him leave. *Don't get involved.*

His eyes softened with amusement. "Thanks, even though you don't know anything about me I'll accept your lie with grace."

"It's not a lie. From what I just saw..." She trailed off thinking of Andrea wondering how her father would have treated her if she'd fallen because she was scared. The little girl's clothes were nicely pressed, her black hair parted into two large braids that ended with purple ribbons that matched her shoes. She was well cared for, and clearly loved. "You'd be surprised. Not all fathers are like you. That's a compliment by the way." Time to go. She didn't like how his eyes met hers. She was not doing this again. Simon had seemed lost too. But he hadn't been. He'd had all that he'd needed. She'd fooled herself into believing that he needed her. Or even wanted her.

His phone rang and he saw the number and said, "Ships sailing in the seas," in a manner that sounded like a swear word. He began furiously texting. "I didn't pay attention to the time. I have to go."

"Right, of course." Minah was prepared to see them go but the little girl kept hold of her hand so that was the only reason she offered to walk them back downstairs, saying she needed to check her mail when she didn't need to.

They stepped out of the elevator and someone said his name. He turned, looking guilty. "I'm so sorry," he said to the striking woman marching towards them.

"Why am I not surprised?" she said in an indulgent tone. She held out her hand to Minah. "He texted me about what happened. He always—"

"We should go," he said firmly, "Thanks again."

The woman didn't seem eager to go just yet. "Has he told you he's a walking disaster?" Her gaze fell on the little girl, "I mean oh my god," she sent him a quick glance, "did you do her hair? It looks a mess. Let me fix it for you." She moved towards the child. The girl frowned and moved back.

Minah didn't know the dynamics and didn't want to intervene but didn't take kindly to criticizing a child who looked perfectly fine, especially about her hair.

She bent down and whispered to her, "You are a wonderfully brave girl and your hair looks lovely."

She smiled then shouted, "Daddy can I—"

The woman jumped and he looked at the little girl startled and quickly said, "Inside voice."

The child lowered her voice to a whisper. "Can I stay with her and you come back and get me?"

He sent a hesitant look at his companion and an apologetic one to Minah.

"No, because that would be rude to both Aunty Leena who has planned this special night for us and Ms. Tate."

The child frowned.

"Maybe another time," Minah said to soften the girl's disappointment then waved her goodbyes without meeting his eyes (too tempting) or the eyes of his companion (she'd suffered enough daggers for one evening, thank you) and left.

Alone in the elevator, Minah felt both heavy and light. She wished she hadn't given him her number (it made her hopeful), but since he'd given her his, it had only seemed polite, right?

She didn't expect him to call. And he didn't.

Not the next day anyway.

Or the following day, but her phone did ring that night...

LEFT UNSAID

LEFT UNSAID

THEY DIDN'T WANT to be there but neither had the courage to admit it. So, the man in the khakis and grey dress shirt and the woman in the A-line black skirt, purple satin blouse, and matching scarf ordered their meal as they usually did when they had their scheduled 'date night' and pretended that everything was fine, although it wasn't.

It was horribly, terribly wrong.

However, no one in the restaurant would have noticed it. The couple blended easily among the low din of voices, the solid wood plank table, catching the fading light of the sun's rays, housing the two spicy halibut and roasted vegetable dishes they'd ordered. And had left barely touched.

Their marriage of sixteen years had produced two children, which they both tolerated more than loved, and their careers had given them the security and status they'd both been raised to expect and revere.

Which they did with gusto. They pretended everything was okay.

When it was truly horribly wrong.

They scheduled date night at least four times a year like one would a performance review. They always went out to dinner—neither wanted to bother with the hassle of scheduling any other activity—and dined at the same restaurant: the Blue Mango. They didn't really talk about anything. There was no need, they really didn't have much to say to each other anymore and they both feared that if they did talk too much, if they really said what was on their mind they'd reveal too much and pour gasoline on their perfect life where the lighted match of one careless word could set it on fire.

Too much was at stake to say anything of importance, so they found it best not to say anything at all.

A young woman with large ears stopped at the table. They knew her as one of the waitresses who'd served them many other times when they came to the restaurant, this evening they'd been assigned someone else but had barely noticed. "Excuse me," she said with a nervous grin, "Hi, it's great to see you both."

The wife and husband plastered on matching plastic smiles and mutely nodded in feigned harmony.

"I'm sorry," she continued, "I know it's none of my business. It's just you come here a lot and..." She bit her lip. "I can't help but notice..." She cleared her throat, sighed, let her gaze fall on the woman's scarf then shifted away before she said in a rush, "You really should get that checked if you haven't already."

They didn't have to pretend not to know what she was talking about; it had been at the table with them. It had been with them for several months now and neither wanted to address it. It was too scary.

But now...now this waitress had given it life by noticing it.

"Thank you," the wife began to say, grateful for the woman's kindness but the husband sliced through her words with a curt, "She's fine."

The startled woman nodded embarrassed and left.

The wife scraped her fork against the plate, carefully pushing her food around, secretly delighting in the twitch of pained annoyance she noticed in her husband's tightened jaw before she stopped. 'She's fine' How long has she been pretending she was fine? How long has she pretended that everything was as she wanted it to be? How long has she pretended to smile at her husband when she really wanted to drag her nails down his face and watch him bleed?

She'd pretended not to notice the puzzled look on her ten-year-old's face when he started to notice the growth on her neck (but was wise enough to say nothing, because saying nothing was how they kept their family in order). She'd pretended not to mind the need to start wearing scarves, or the disquiet she'd felt when she'd briefly—casually—mentioned if she should get it checked and her husband accusing her of vanity.

Was it vanity? She didn't want to be a burden. That's how he made her feel. That if something was wrong it would be a burden to him, to the children. What else was she for? How dare she expect special treatment.

That's what they didn't talk about: That her death would be more an inconvenience than anything else.

The wife took a bite of the halibut the spiciness making her lips burn, and her tongue tingle. She cleared her throat. "Maybe she's right and I should—"

"It will go down with time," the husband said. "I'm sure with some meditation and stress reduction techniques you can deal with it."

"But—"

"You always like to make a drama of things, don't you?"

The wife stared at the husband stunned. It was the first time in a long time he'd managed to make her feel anything but boredom or anger. This sensation of surprise was rare.

The feeling shook her awake from a long sleep.

She realized this was a moment of choice. Did she look out for herself, dare to make a decision for herself, or continue to pretend?

Perhaps he was right and it would go away, but if it didn't?

If it didn't...? What did that mean? For her? For him? For them?

How could three words linger with the acrid scent of dread, the bitter taste of despair? Cause one's skin to tingle with the prickly sensation of sorrow, uncertainty, fear? And why was this unnamed situation somehow her fault? Why didn't he care to ask her if it was uncomfortable? If it hurt?

But she'd lose so much if she left him. His job provided her health insurance.

She depended on him for too much.

The wife took a deep breath and stared down at the table as she tried to gather courage. "I will see someone—"

"No," the husband said. "You're fine."

It was the tone this time that caused her to look up at him startled. He didn't sound certain. For the first time, he sounded afraid.

"You're fine," he said again, he kept his gaze lowered, his hand steady as he pushed rice onto his fork. "You just need to rest."

She stared at him, her heart pounding. She'd never thought that he was pretending too. She'd never thought all this time he'd been pretending not to care but now she saw that he did because he continued to carefully push the rice...grain by grain...onto his fork as he had on the day he'd asked her to be exclusive. He'd said the words so cavalierly that she hadn't been sure he'd meant it. He'd always been guarded with his emotions. Careful. Then she remembered his sister telling her that they'd dealt with a lot of loss and he tried not to get too attached.

And that had started weighing on her over the years that he'd kept her at a distance.

Polite, considerate, routine.

She wondered if she mattered to him.

She said his name softly. The motion stopped but he didn't look up at her.

"I want to get it checked. It's probably nothing."

She saw his jaw twitch, the grip on his utensils tightened. And what if it's not? His actions seemed to say.

He carefully set the utensils down. "I'm a coward." He lifted his gaze to meet hers. "I don't want to know."

She felt tears because it had been so long since he'd really looked at her—and saw a whole person, not a label, not a role, but a person with a past and a personality, which she'd allowed the roles to smother—and she realized the same. It had been so long since she'd really looked at him.

They'd allowed themselves to become strangers to each other but the fear, the naked vulnerability in his gaze reminded her of why she'd married him.

She wiped her face, surprised by the sudden soft stream of tears, and couldn't stop a smile, feeling both vulnerable and strong. "Me too. I'm scared."

He closed his eyes. "Why couldn't it be me?"

She covered his hand and said his name.

He furrowed his brows, bit his lip.

She said his name again.

He looked at her.

She nodded to his plate. "Finish your food. You've hardly touched it."

"Same with you."

"I wasn't sure you still loved me."

"I wasn't sure either," he said and chuckled at her look of surprise. He shrugged. "I was going through the motions. I took so much for granted. I admit that. But then when I saw..." His brown gaze darted to her neck and quickly flew away again, "then I got afraid and I'm sorry I pushed you away but it felt better than the thought of losing you."

She sighed. "I know."

"I'd started to feel that I couldn't feel anything, that I was stuck in a life that was familiar but wasn't exactly mine. One day I asked our oldest how his day was, and he looked at me shocked. Not bored, not mildly attentive but shocked. I asked him what was wrong, and he said it was the first time I'd directly asked him a question in a year. I wanted to argue or explain but I didn't and strangely, he told me what he was working on. And I thought this kid is interesting how come I didn't know that? Suddenly everything started to matter more. I realized all the time that had passed. The moments I hadn't noticed, and I wanted to notice everything except..."

"Yes."

"So, I didn't."

"But we won't anymore," she said, determined to make a doctor's appointment.

He took a deep breath. "Let's pack this up and order dessert."

She grinned. That really wasn't like him. "Okay."

No more waiting for the right moment, the correct time. No more pretending, they'd change.

They'd take pleasure in life again.

Savor every bite.

Together.

As one.

WAITING ON YESTERDAY

WAITING ON YESTERDAY

Of course, he wasn't coming.

She was being stood up on a blind date, after spending money getting her hair done (into shoulder-length twists), buying a new silk dress (a soft peach-colored one with flowy sleeves) and matching shoes, plus a handbag she didn't need.

She'd succumbed because the sales clerk seemed to need the commission and Alana felt a little sorry for her, so she'd bought the circular-shaped bag that couldn't carry more than three items—a tube of lipstick, an ID card and a paper clip, if lucky. But since she needed to carry more than three minuscule items, she'd left the overpriced handbag at home and brought her regular one, which could hide a brick and possibly even a lampshade.

But the unnecessary handbag purchase and the

date that showed all signs of not coming would be a suitable end to a terrible week.

A week so miserable that if a large asteroid had managed to hit the Caribbean restaurant, smashed it into smithereens and created a crater the size of an Olympic stadium, which would probably have been an improvement.

She'd given her date a half hour to make a belated appearance. That was more than enough time, right? She'd texted him and gotten no reply.

Not that he was a stranger to her. They'd been chatting online for two months and it had felt as if they'd had a connection. He'd even been the one to initiate their meeting in person. That had been a good sign, right?

But then Alana had a sneaking suspicion she'd scared him off with two words. Two words that shouldn't have been an issue but could be when moving from the beautiful virtual realm of online intimacy to the harsh glare of real life. Few relationships seemed to make that leap smoothly.

She'd hoped theirs would have been different.

After setting up a date, time, and location to meet (Saturday, 6:00 pm at the Blue Mango restaurant—his suggestion, not hers) he'd teasingly asked who he should look for. And she'd innocently replied: *The black woman wearing a pink choker.*

Suddenly there was a pause. The kind of pause you notice. A pause that had all the impact of a gigantic boulder rolling down a mountain and landing in the center of a creek, damming up what had once flowed freely (their banter, their feelings, their silly emojis) to an aching trickle.

Alana remembered holding her phone (holding her breath really), wondering why it was taking him so long to reply. She wondered if she was imagining the length of it. Maybe it was nothing. Maybe a moment could feel like an eternity.

But when eternity started to feel like infinity, she nudged him with a smile emoji (Of course. Didn't want to appear pushy) and texted:

Are you still there?

No smile back. Just the response: *Yeah, sorry. Okay, see you then.*

What do you look like?

Don't worry. I'll find you.

Except she should have worried. Because he wasn't there and she knew he had no intention of finding her.

She tugged on her choker with restless fingers before she lifted up her water glass, the ice long melted, then set it back down with a sigh. It wasn't as if she'd catfished him or anything. She just...forgot. She knew he worked at a community college and he knew she worked at a company that provided eyeglass accessories. They'd gotten friendly on a forum that talked about orchids of all things.

She'd felt a connection when he'd said he saw orchids as a metaphor for life. Soon they were going to virtual orchid events and flower shows, watching movies, and playing games. For nearly two months she'd felt she'd found someone special and when he said he wanted to meet her she hadn't hesitated.

But she should have.

Because...she'd forgotten the power of two words. Or really just one—black.

She'd forgotten that being black mattered when she really wished it didn't. His race wouldn't matter but hers definitely would. She hated that she actually felt a little guilty for not warning him.

She even hated that she thought she had to 'warn' anyone. Why did she have to feel as if every online to offline transition had to have the same gravity as admitting one had a venereal disease? *Full disclosure: my melanin is on the darker spectrum. I hope that's okay and won't completely destroy all the fun we've had and make you think less of me.*

And what kind of emoji would one put on the end of a statement like that, so it didn't sound embarrassingly confessional? Or aggressive or pathetic?

But perhaps she should have made sure to tell him first because then she wouldn't be sitting alone on this spring evening, occasionally looking out the rain-streaked window where she saw a mud-spattered orange Acura parked across the street, resembling a large pumpkin just pulled out of a soggy field. Of course, thinking of pumpkins only reminded her that she was no Cinderella. But staring out the window made it easier to ignore the savory scent of spices and herbs that floated through the restaurant, the hum of conversation punctuated by bursts of laughter and the heavy weight of the empty seat in front of her.

She didn't want to catch anyone's eye and she was determined not to check the time—again. She already had a sense another ten minutes had gone by.

She'd given him forty minutes.

Stupid to even wait this long, making an appetizer of stuffed plantain cups—a heady mixture of shredded chicken and spicy mayo—last, as if the seven miniature items were a full-course meal. She'd left two of them sitting on the white square plate not wanting to give the anxious waitress a reason to clear the plate and ask if she was ready to order. When in truth she knew the waitress wanted to clear the table for someone more worthy. Alana didn't blame her.

But she still made no move to leave. She felt like staying just to make the cost of her new hairstyle matter (she usually wore it up), the dress a good splurge (she hadn't bought a new dress in years), and because she wanted to matter even if it was as an irritant.

Plus, if she stretched out the evening she wouldn't have to deal with Brenda. She knew exactly what her best friend, who never lacked for dates (even in high school) and was now in a happy long-term relationship with a man she'd met online, would say: "Didn't I tell you it wasn't worth it? Women like us cannot be wasting our time on these other platforms. I don't care how popular they are. If you want to feel desired and admired, you stick with Caribbean Cool or sites like it."

Alana knew her friend had a point but didn't want to admit that she hadn't had success there either. She didn't just want Caribbean men or men interested in Caribbean women because, at thirty-two, she felt as Caribbean as a bag of vinegar potato crisps and Buffalo wings, thanks to moving from Jamaica to the US when she was five years old. She'd been a disappointment one too many times. She wasn't exotic enough for some guys, too exotic for others.

Of course, Brenda never had to know about this non-date. Her friend had been underwhelmed by Alana's orchid-loving teacher anyway, always nudging her to find out more and figure out what he looked like. But Alana told her she didn't care what he looked like because she'd felt they'd made a soul connection. Brenda had laughed at that one, and now, looking back, perhaps her friend had a right to. Soul connections didn't exist.

Perhaps she'd lie to her friend and say that she was the one who didn't show up, but Alana was terrible at lying and after getting over her friend's 'I told you so' perhaps she'd help her laugh about it.

Alana sighed and picked up one of the stuffed plantain cups, that had arrived at the table crispy and hot but now felt cold, contemplating whether she should order something else (she was hungry and if the appetizers were any indication, the food would be delicious) or leave and grab a takeaway before heading home.

She made the mistake of glancing at the other patrons to see what they were eating, but instead saw an older man gazing tenderly at an older woman; two middle-aged women enjoyed their Caribbean coleslaw; a young girl giggled at something her male companion said, a group of four guys joked with each other. Everyone looked natural and happy. And here she was all alone with a cold appetizer. She'd give the poor waitress, a dark-skinned cutie who'd been very attentive forty minutes ago and whose cheery smile had begun to wane, the table so that she could get a better patron. Takeaway it is.

Alana reached down to grab her handbag when she heard the chair in front of her scrape against the floor. She guessed it was the waitress asking if she could clear the table.

"Yes," Alana said surprised by how tired and sad her own voice sounded. "I'm just about to—"

She glanced up and nearly choked on her words. There was no waitress. Just a large, serious-looking man (who looked to be in his mid-to-late thirties) dressed in a blue dress shirt and dark jacket. He wore black square glasses and looked like he wouldn't be able to distinguish an orchid from a dandelion.

His dark brown eyes seemed to be only a shade lighter than his cocoa skin. He was the kind of man who usually scared her—she didn't do 'serious.' Serious guys were too intense for her liking. Give her carefree any day.

She would have grabbed her handbag and left (she wasn't going to waste another minute on a man who wore expensive glasses but couldn't be bothered to iron his shirt. It had more wrinkles than a shar-pei) if he hadn't looked so flustered.

"I'm so sorry I'm late," he said in a deep tone that sounded sincere. "I didn't think you'd still be here."

"Probably shouldn't be," she mumbled.

"What?"

She shook her head. "Never mind."

He slid a hand down his face, grabbed the water glass closest to him, and finished it in one long swallow before he looked around to get the waitress's attention. But she was busy flirting with the four young men and didn't notice.

"You can have mine," Alana said, handing him the glass. "I haven't touched it."

"Thanks," he said, and his large hand covered hers with such shocking warmth she nearly dropped the glass. He quickly released her hand and the glass fell to the wooden table with a thud splashing a little.

"Sorry," they said in unison then laughed uneasily. Alana mopped up the tiny spill with her napkin.

"Let's try this again," she said then pushed the glass over to him.

He took it and drank half of it before setting it down again.

This was awful. She'd waited forty minutes for this? For this solemn, dehydrated man?

He wasn't anywhere close to how she'd imagined him to be. She knew that people could be a little bit different in real life but he seemed like a different person. Online he was always ready with a joke, very witty, loved to talk. The one thing she'd been looking forward to was seeing his smile.

She doubted this man knew how to. She half imagined that his face would crack if he tried. He only knew how to offer apologies and drink water like her cousin Carl downing pints at an open bar.

"You wouldn't believe the week I've had," he said.

Alana felt her temper rise. Really? He was going to arrive late and then make this all about him? "Why didn't you respond to my text?"

"Did I mention my mobile's broken? I really didn't think you'd still be here. But never mind, you're here and I'm glad. You must be starving. Do you know what you want?"

She hesitated. She detected the hint of an accent but he spoke so fast she couldn't pin it down. And why was he asking her what she wanted to eat? Was he one of those guys who would try to order for her? Or tell her what was best?

"Yes," she said.

He leaned back with a sigh of relief. "Great. I'll leave it to you then. Order two."

She narrowed her eyes unsure. "But you don't know what I'm going to have."

"As long as it's edible, I'll eat it." He lifted his hand to get the waitress's attention then realized her attention was still elsewhere and would likely stay there for awhile. "Excuse me," he said before he stood and walked over to the young woman who was playfully fanning herself with her tablet.

Alana watched the waitress jump in surprise when he spoke up behind her. The young woman spun around and stared up at him—whether in fear or awe, she couldn't tell—as he motioned to Alana. The waitress quickly nodded before he turned and returned to the table. Before Alana could ask him what he'd said to her, the waitress hurried over to them and said in a breathless rush her gaze fixed on Alana's date, "So you know what you want?"

He nodded towards Alana. "Yes, we're ready to order."

It took the waitress a moment to realize that 'we' meant Alana and it was a good delay since she'd lied. She opened up the menu and quickly scanned it as he watched her. Was this a test, a challenge?

"Would you like an appetizer?" she asked him as a way to stall.

"If it will stop me from eating my fist, then yes."

He said the words in such a deadpan way she wasn't sure he was joking so she bit back a laugh. She glanced down to look at his hands but saw they were hidden under the table. Not that she needed a reminder, she knew they were as large as the rest of him and she tried not to remember the warmth of his palm when it covered her hand. "Another order of stuffed plantain cups and plantain with halibut," she said then immediately regretted her choice. Plantain again? What was she thinking? What kind of impression would that make? At this rate, she'd probably order banana ice cream with plantain flakes.

"Baked or fried?" the waitress asked.

Alana quickly looked over at her date. He stared back, his expression blank, giving her no indication of his preference. Her heart sank. Why was she doing this? She could go home now. She didn't have to order. There was time to change her mind. She didn't want to spend another minute with this man.

The waitress cleared her throat. "Bake or fried?"

She'd stay for the food, not the company. It was at least worth that. "Baked, please."

Her date spoke up and added, "And could you send over two more glasses of water and tea when the meal is ready. And for the lady..." He looked at her in question.

Alana stared back in amazement. Did he have a hollow leg, a second stomach? How could a man consume so much liquid?

"N-nothing," she said, "thank you." Once the waitress left, she said, "Have you finished running a marathon or something?"

"Or something sounds about right."

But he didn't. Sound right, that is. His speech pattern was all wrong. Well, not wrong but different. She couldn't help but compare it to how he 'sounded' online. More cordial, clever, easygoing. In person his words were unremarkable but the way he said them made them seem interesting (was it the odd accent she still couldn't quite place?). He didn't look anything like the way she'd imagined. He didn't sound like himself but he had shown up. Perhaps she could salvage the evening after all even if she never planned to see him again.

"Let's compare notes," he said.

She frowned. "Notes?"

"On who's had the worst week."

She nodded. "Oh, you're competitive, hmm? Truly it isn't a game I'd want to win, but I'm sure I would."

"You won't." He took off his glasses and lowered his gaze.

"Stop!" she said when she saw him reach for the hem of his jacket.

He looked up at her startled and she saw that the glasses were an improvement. He should wear them. Always. Otherwise, he could freeze people in place. She'd never seen someone with such penetrating dark eyes. She felt like a poor butterfly pinned to a corkboard. But once she recovered from how intense his gaze was, she realized he was curious. That he was really looking at her, as if what she was about to say was important. She'd never had that happen before.

She swallowed. "You cannot clean your glasses with your clothes." She opened her handbag and pretended to search inside as an excuse not to look at him. "The fabric's too harsh and can scratch the surface of your lens. I have extra lens cloths you can use."

"Why?"

She paused. Was he being obtuse on purpose? Did she have to remind him what she did for a living? Then again, few people in her field could rattle off the benefits of self-moistening lens cloths, the pleasure of ear cushions to gain pressure relief and how carefully crafted eyeglass caddies could display one's lenses in style, the way Alana could. Her family liked to joke she was wedded to the job, which wasn't something to brag about. "It's a hobby of mine." She handed him the cloth.

"Thanks."

"So, what are the stakes?"

He frowned puzzled. "Stakes?" he said while he gently, rhythmically rubbed the cloth over his lens in a way that was oddly...calming. Most people quickly cleaned their lenses, but he took a more careful and methodic approach, stroking them like they were a treasured pet, which she found alluring. Perhaps his serious nature wasn't so bad after all.

"Yes," she said, reluctantly pulling her gaze away

from his hands, "the person with the worst week gets what? They should at least get something."

He rubbed his chin, looking as focused as if she'd asked him to calculate the dimensions of a rocket ship. "You're right. That's a good question. What would you want?"

"Aside from going back in time and making sure it never happened?"

He slid his glasses back on his face and she detected the hint of a smile. "Yes, aside from that."

She'd gotten him to smile? A little? That was a win. Maybe with a little more teasing, she'd get him to be like he was online. "How about never being born? Think that's possible?"

He shook his head while he carefully folded up the lens cloth. He placed it in his pocket. "I'm sure your week couldn't have been that bad."

"If you think so then I've already won."

He clasped his hands together before he said, "Go on then, surprise me."

"Okay." Alana rubbed her hands together and cracked her knuckles as if preparing for a fight. She was going to take him down. She took a deep breath ready to dazzle him with her woes when the waitress returned with their appetizers and two waters. She watched as he readily made three of the plantain cups disappear before he motioned for her to continue.

"Okay. I—"

"Do you want some?"

"No."

"Are you sure?"

She pointed to the two cold leftovers. "This is what I was munching on while I was waiting for you."

She expected him to have the grace to look embarrassed instead he looked pleased. Before she could ask why he said, "Right. Sorry. Go on."

She cleared her throat. "It started on Monday when my roommate got upset with her boss and decided to take out her anger on the bookshelf."

"I think I know where this is going."

"I don't think you do. Because this bookshelf was put together by a man who refused to read instructions, so it toppled and all the books on it crashed to the ground, followed by the entire structure knocking over Tad, Rad, and Lad."

He frowned "You've lost me."

"My three clownfish," she clarified. She was sure she'd mentioned them before.

"Oh, I'm sorry."

"Their tank fell with a mighty crash and they flopped along the ground fighting to breathe. I managed to catch Lad and Rad but it was too late for Tad. He slipped under the couch and by the time I got to him..." She let her words fade and took a deep breath.

"I'm surprised you could tell them apart."

"Are you making fun of me?"

He leaned back and folded his arms. "I wouldn't dare."

"So, he didn't make it. That was Monday. Tuesday my roommate—" She paused when she glanced down and saw that all the appetizers had disappeared including the other two leftovers. "Wow, you were hungry."

"You have no idea," he said in a deep voice. "Tell me about Tuesday."

It took her a moment to refocus because not only did the tone of his voice seem to hide multitudes, making her wonder what he meant, but his eyes did too. She couldn't get over how he studied her. No one could find her this interesting. "Right...um...where was I? No, don't tell me. It was Tuesday. That's when my roommate decided to put the bookshelf up herself and a board fell on her foot and she ended up with a foot fracture."

"Sounds like her week was worse than yours."

"Did I mention that she's my cousin and that her mother called me up and scolded me for about thirty minutes about the accident that was suddenly *my* fault? And then my mother did the same and then her boyfriend?"

"I get the point."

"And then her daughter—"

"She lives with you too?"

"No, she lives with her father, but she was very upset I wasn't able to save Lad."

"I thought it was Tad."

"That's what I said."

He rubbed his chin, and if she wasn't mistaken, he looked like he was trying to hide a smile. "Right. So that's Tuesday."

"Wednesday was the minor incident of losing my job—"

His brows shot up. "That's minor?"

"—to the guy I'd trained for the position."

He winced. "Sorry."

"I should have seen it coming."

"Son of the owner?"

"Yes."

"What are you going to do?"

"Not much I can do. My mother's always favored him."

He nodded in sympathy. "Yes, well that's...Wait. What? Did you say *mother*?"

"Oh, did I skip over the part of the company being a family business that I've worked in since I was sixteen and the one that my brother ignored until after he 'found himself' on a walkabout in Australia and decided to return home with a wife and three step-kids under the age of three?"

He frowned. "Is that even possible?"

"It is when you marry someone who'd just had triplets." She pointed at him. "Don't grin, I'm not joking."

"You're making this up."

"I wish I were."

"So let me get this straight. So far you have a cousin with a fractured foot, a dead fish, and a brother who pushed you out of a job."

"That's right. Have I won yet?"

He looked at her for a long moment then said, "Is that the end of your week?"

"Not yet."

"Then we'll see."

That intrigued her. Could his week really have been worse than that?

Alana opened her handbag. "This will seem trivial to you, but I'll show you anyway." She pulled out a silver and black tube of lipstick and took off the top to reveal a tiny misshapen mound of reddish purple. "For fifteen years this has been my savior. No matter how low I feel, in an instant, it makes me feel better."

He gently took the lipstick tube from her and frowned at the stub left. "Did it stop working or something?"

"It's being discontinued."

"Oh," he said trying to appear empathetic but looked confused instead.

"I know you don't understand. You're probably thinking this is merely purple face paint. But to me, it's a touch of raisin with a hint of blueberry that complements my skin tone. You have no idea how many shades of lipstick say they are for 'all' shades and really aren't."

"I'm sorry," he said, and he sounded like he meant it. His gaze dipped to her lips with the softness of a featherlike caress before meeting her gaze again.

Alana took the lipstick from him, her lips feeling as if they'd just been kissed, resisting the urge to bite her lips. She fought to maintain a light tone as if she didn't wonder what he would taste like; how his lips would feel against hers. "Once it's gone it'll be gone forever." She dropped the lipstick tube back into her handbag with a casual nonchalance she didn't feel. She wouldn't mention that when she'd learned about it being discontinued, she'd actually burst into tears. "And that's it for me. Except—" She stopped unsure she should continue.

"Except?"

"I went on this blind date and the guy showed up forty minutes late and arrived wearing a wrinkled shirt."

He sniffed in disgust. "And you waited for him?"

"Well, he finally showed up, didn't he?"

He frowned. "Does that matter?"

She frowned back. "Don't you think so? You came and this date hasn't been too awful."

He blinked. "I don't know what you're talking about."

"I'm talking about you coming here in an unironed shirt forty minutes late."

He opened his mouth, closed it. Looked down at his shirt then scratched his cheek perplexed. "I really don't know what you're on about," he said his words more accented than before. She found it to be an odd Manchester (England) Brooklyn (America) mashup. "First of all, this shirt *is* ironed. It's the fabric that makes it look this way. It's a style. My sister thought it would improve my chances and...never mind." He shook his head as if trying to gather his thoughts. "I'd never let anyone wait for me that long. Especially someone—" He stopped and bit his lip then said, "Not a chance."

"But you just did."

"When?"

"Tonight."

"I was ten minutes late."

"We agreed to meet at six o'clock."

"No," he said drawing out the word, "it was six-thirty."

She reached for her mobile. "I have proof."

"I don't need proof, Mellodie, I remember the time."

"That's not—" Alana paused. "Wait, did you just call me Mellodie?"

He grinned. Fully and completely. His grin was beautiful and engaging, revealing a man she wanted to know better and the sight of it made her want to weep. "Aren't I allowed to?" he said. "I thought we were on a first-name basis."

Alana put her cell phone away, her mind racing.

This truly was the worst week. He thought she was someone else?

He stared at her concerned. "Are you okay?"

"Well, I—"

He stopped and his gaze shifted to something behind her. "Ah," he said sounding relieved, "the man who brought us together. Drake Henson."

She turned and saw an imposing-looking man with black and grey fighting for dominance in his hair. But what made her heart race wasn't the fact that the owner of the restaurant was coming over to them, she'd read a little bit about him online, but rather the confused look on his fierce face.

This was all wrong. This interesting man had come to the wrong table. What would happen when he found out the truth? She couldn't face another rejection. She didn't want to see the warm welcoming expression leave her companion's face. They would become strangers again just when she'd allowed herself to hope, just when she'd started to think that perhaps serious men with deadpan humor might be more interesting than she thought. But once he knew the truth, she wouldn't matter to him.

She was sick of not mattering.

Alana jumped up and grabbed her handbag. "Forgive me. I'm so so sorry." She rushed towards the door just as she overheard the Henson guy say, "Who was that?"

SHE RAN ALL the way to the metro station, even though she knew no one was chasing after her. Thankfully, the station was only a few blocks away because she wasn't a runner, her heels weren't designed for running, and there were tiny puddles on the rain-soaked pavement that she kept stepping into.

Once she reached the station, she gripped the escalator railing and descended into the dark tunnel at a pace so slow that for a moment she wondered if she was moving at all. The only thing that seemed to be moving was the river of tears streaming down her face. She tried to wipe them away but more kept coming as regret clawed at her broken heart.

She should have left when she'd had the chance. Then she'd never have met him. If she hadn't been so hopeful he wouldn't have mistaken her for someone else.

Someone else.

That was the worst part of the week. Every day there had been a moment when she'd wanted to be someone else. Someone who didn't get scolded, someone who was a parent's favorite, someone more ideal when it came to looks, someone more ideal in general.

Someone—anyone—besides herself.

She felt bad for leaving him with the bill. She'd call later and pay for something else. Since he was friends with the owner, she figured he would get the message somehow. She silently swore. She didn't even know his name! But she'd be able to describe him. That would be enough.

Alana made it to the train level and raced inside a metro car just before the doors were about to close. A guy with size fourteen shoes stepped on her foot and didn't notice.

Alana closed her eyes, wishing herself far away.

STRANGELY, her bad week came in the middle of a good month. Her roommate/cousin decided to move out to live with her boyfriend. She got another position in the family business, in the product management division, and, best of all, she forgot about him.

Well, at least she stopped thinking of him every minute of every hour. She'd gone through half a day without thinking of him. That was progress. (She'd named him Dante because he looked like a Dante, and she imagined him as a financial analyst who liked to take photographs on his weekly hikes).

Brenda had wanted all the gory details of her humiliation. Alana offered her the abridged version. No need to mention the way his skin felt when his hand covered hers, the look in his eyes when his gaze dipped to her lips, the hard-earned smile that appeared with all the warmth of a summer sun cresting over a blue sea, the way he really listened as if he found her interesting.

Two months later she felt ready to buy a companion for Rad and Lad.

On a hot Saturday afternoon, Alana found herself standing in an aisle bracketed by rows of clear glass and water, free of even a speck of algae, as she looked at large fish tanks. She knew the independent pet store prided itself on its attention to detail and external filtration systems. She turned to look at another selection when she saw him. He was unmistakably dressed in dark jeans and a light-colored jacket. She'd briefly wondered if she'd imagined him but he was just as she'd remembered.

He hadn't noticed her. He was focused on the large tank in front of him, watching a school of neon fish freely swim past him, as if captivated by their bright red and blue stripes. Then he glanced down at something on the floor. If she ran, he wouldn't—

He glanced up and saw her. She froze.

Still time to run. He was far enough away. Or perhaps he didn't remember her? Perhaps he'd pretend not to notice her. She'd had that happen before.

"Hey," he said, and she took a step back ready to turn. "Don't run."

It was more than a demand. Or even a command. It was a warning: If you run, I will catch you.

Alana took a deep breath and stared at the ground. No running. Fine. She'd face this. She'd endure a couple of awkward minutes and then it would be over.

She felt more than heard him approach. She couldn't meet his gaze, so she fumbled in her bag for her mobile. "I'm so sorry I left you with the bill," she said pulling out her phone and unlocking it, "If you tell me how much—"

He gently covered her hand. She felt the same heat, wondered if it was partly embarrassment or something more.

"Are you looking for Tad's replacement?"

She looked up sharply. "Tad could never be replaced."

"Of course."

"You...remember?"

He shoved his hands in his jacket pockets. "It's sort of hard to forget when a woman runs out on you."

"But you know why, right?"

"Because you're not Mellodie."

She nodded.

"Why didn't you just tell me who you were?"

"Because I didn't want you to be disappointed. Once your friend cleared up the misunderstanding you—"

"I would have laughed and then told you what my week had been like."

"But...you came there to be with Mellodie."

"Who clearly wasn't there. Instead, I met someone else."

"Right."

"And I was enjoying her company until she ran away."

He'd enjoyed her company? Alana tried to read the situation. Did that mean he wasn't mad? Perhaps she hadn't completely ruined this chance. Since he'd paid for dinner perhaps, she could return the favor.

She cleared her dry throat. "I'd like to make it up to you so—"

The sound of his cell phone alerting him to a text, which strangely sounded like the theme song from *Jaws*, interrupted her. "Sorry," he said, quickly texting back a reply. "Give me a second."

Alana looked at his phone in dismay. "But I don't want to keep you if—"

"It's okay." He tucked his phone away. "So, are you getting another clownfish?"

"I still can't believe you remembered," Alana said touched.

He held her gaze. "It was a memorable night."

"Oh Sean, there you are," a woman said, coming up behind him.

Sean? He didn't look like a Sean. But she really didn't know much about him except how he'd made her feel for one night.

He turned to the woman with pecan skin and a stylish bob haircut and said, "I'll be with you in a minute."

She tugged on his jacket sleeve in a familiar way

and a teasing smile touched her pretty lips. "I'd wondered where you'd disappeared to." She glanced around and sniffed. "What a strange place for you to end up. I thought after what had happened you wouldn't want another pet. Or is it because—"

"I was just looking," he said.

"I don't mind helping you—"

"Mellodie, it's okay. I'm fine," he added in a firm voice.

It wasn't his voice that Alana noticed. It was the name he said.

Mellodie.

Mellodie who didn't look like she'd ever have to worry about her lipstick being discontinued. Who probably only had good weeks. Who was likely the youngest child of parents who adored her.

Alana shifted her gaze and noticed him—Sean— studying her. To fill the silence she said, "I see you two finally caught up."

He nodded, but his expression gave nothing away. At least he didn't pity her.

And they looked happy and cozy, and she'd lost her chance. It was her fault. She had no one else to blame. If she hadn't run, perhaps they would have come to this pet store together instead. She sighed. Saying "Can we be friends?" sounded sort of sad and she really didn't just want to be friends. He'd always be a reminder of where cowardice got you.

Mellodie playfully nudged him. "This is where you introduce us."

Sean blinked and cleared his throat, seeming to come to himself. "Right. Sorry. Mellodie this is..." He turned to her. Alana knew he was waiting for her to offer her name since he didn't know it but she didn't want to give it. He'd forget it anyway.

"Nobody," she said with a laugh that sounded harsh even to her own ears. "Absolutely nobody." He opened his mouth as if he were about to argue so she quickly said, "I'm sorry I caused you any trouble. I'm glad things worked out for you. Goodbye."

She turned and left the shop without a new fish instead bearing the weight of a twice broken heart.

"You still could have invited him for coffee or something," Brenda said later that day as they sat on Alana's couch and ate Samoas.

"No, I couldn't," Alana mumbled around the crunchy cookie. "I hope I never see him again. Just the thought of him makes my skin burn."

"With desire?"

"With volcanic level embarrassment. I must look so pathetic. I feel pathetic."

The original orchid-loving guy she was supposed to meet had ghosted her. No surprise there. He clearly was as much a coward as she was.

She was tired of being a coward.

So that Monday Alana made a change. She left the family business (for a while) and took a break to reassess her role in it. Her mother called her almost every day reminding her of her duty, legacy, and responsibility. She reminded her mother that she had the fortitude to have other children to maintain her legacy so there was no worry. Then her mother finally admitted that she wanted her back because the morale in the department her brother was in charge of had dipped since he'd taken over.

Alana listened and said nothing.

Her mother told her that she'd give her more money.

Alana listened and still said nothing.

Until her mother asked if she wanted her former position, with a pay rise and more autonomy, and she said 'yes'.

Her brother would work with her unless he felt the need to leave.

He didn't and actually admitted to feeling relieved that she was in charge again and that he preferred to follow.

It was nice to see her effort rewarded.

It was nice to not want to be someone else.

So, she decided to take herself to the Blue Mango restaurant to celebrate. She arrived wearing a light purple blouse, flowing skirt, and silver dangling earrings. She didn't care that she was alone. She was going to order something different and savor every bite. She didn't need to wait for a special someone.

She was enough.

Alana looked at her menu and thought about ordering spiced chicken when she glanced up and saw Mellodie sitting with Sean at one of the other tables.

Sean sat with his back to her, but Mellodie's profile was clear. Alana didn't remember Sean having an earring but everything else about him—the cut of his hair, the way his jacket draped his broad shoulders, the dark glasses—was the same.

She thought of leaving. Seeing him enjoying his meal with someone else hurt. Even after all these months.

She bent down to pick up her handbag then stopped. She came here to enjoy herself and she would. She didn't have to watch them. If she changed seats, she could even pretend they weren't there.

Pleased with her decision she stood.

"You're not leaving yet, are you?"

"No, just changing—"

She stopped when she saw him. Sean. She glanced behind him and saw Mellodie and Sean. But that was impossible because Sean was here—standing in front of her. She looked at Sean, then the other Sean who, upon closer inspection, not only sported an earring, a possible neck tattoo, and was a shade lighter, but didn't look like Sean at all. Her mind had shown her what she'd expected to see.

"Is something wrong?" he said.

"You're not with Mellodie anymore?"

"Mind if I sit down?"

"No." She took a seat too.

He looked at her glass. She pushed it towards him. He took it and finished it. She noticed he looked just flustered like the first time they'd met, but this time she saw a bead of sweat slide down his face.

"Why are you always so thirsty?"

He shook his head. "I'm not always thirsty."

"Then why are you thirsty now?"

"Because I ran here."

"Why would you do that?"

He sat back and stared at her amused. "You really can't guess?"

"No."

He sighed. "Drake called and told me you were here, and I thought: Why not?"

"You came to see me?"

He lowered his gaze and his voice. "Is that so hard to believe?"

Yes! "What happened between you and...her?"

"Tad."

"What?"

He shrugged. "Once I saw you again at the pet store, I knew I was being unfair to her, so we ended it."

"I'm sorry."

He lifted a brow. "Really?"

She couldn't stop a grin. "No."

He nodded pleased. "Good. Have you ordered yet?"

She shook her head.

He gestured to the menu. "You know the drill."

"Order for both of us?"

He nodded.

After she placed their orders he said, "Well, when we first met, my worst week definitely beat yours. For starters, I had two tenants skip out on rent."

"You're a landlord?"

"I own a small property."

"You're not a financial analyst?"

He furrowed his brow. "Why would I be a financial analyst?"

"Never mind."

"That's strangely specific."

"I know, I just thought you looked like..." She waved her hands. "Never mind. Go on."

"I had a big fight with my father about the tenants and he reminded me that I was too nice and that's why people use me. Then my ex-girlfriend called me up—"

"And told you she was getting married."

"No."

"She'd fallen in love with your best friend."

He sent her a stern look.

She mimed zipping her lips.

"My ex-girlfriend called and said she wanted visiting rights to Callie."

"You have a child?"

"No, I have a dog. And when we broke up, she was fine with me keeping Callie. Then out of the blue, calm as you like, she said she wanted to see her, and I agreed."

"That doesn't sound so bad."

"And that week she decided to kidnap her."

"What do you mean?"

"I mean she disappeared with my dog."

"And what did you do?"

"When I tracked her down, she tearfully told me she'd made a mistake and begged me to let her keep Callie and so I did."

Alana frowned. "Your father's right, you are too nice."

He scratched his ear. "No, not really. I got Callie back the following week."

"How?"

"Told her that I'd send her the bill for Callie's thyroid treatments."

"She's sick?"

He flashed a wicked grin. "No, but she didn't bother to check, as I knew she wouldn't, and she dropped Callie off as quick as she could."

"So, your week wasn't that bad after all."

"Like I said, that only happened afterwards. But the week we're talking about is the one where I had tenants skip out, a fight with my dad, my ex kidnapped my dog and then on top of that I had an old dryer that decided to cook my clothes before dying on me and because of that I made the mistake of asking my sister for help and ended up wearing a shirt that looked like crumbled parchment paper on a blind date. But then when I thought the week couldn't get any worse, I met this amazing woman, and she ran out on me."

Alana felt her face burn. "But you met someone else."

He nodded slowly. "Yes, the woman who'd initially stood me up." He flashed a sour grin. "So that week ended with me being stood up by one woman and deserted by another. A woman I couldn't stop thinking about."

Alana escaped the need of having to reply, thanks to the arrival of their meal. This time she'd ordered yellow rice and jerk chicken, and the food was just as good as she'd hoped it would be.

"Do you know anything about orchids?" she asked Sean after a few delicious bites.

"No...but I'm willing to learn."

"Actually, I'd rather you didn't." And when he sent her a quizzing look, she brushed it aside and said, "A story for another day," then changed the subject to something safe and mundane and not the real questions that swirled in her mind. Such as: Why did Mellodie not show up? How did they get together? What made Mellodie change her mind about him? Why did Sean give her another chance? Did they really break up because of her?

The evening ended too soon for both of them.

They walked outside into the warmth of the summer evening and briefly stood in an awkward silence trying to find the best way to part.

"I'd love to—," Alana said at the same time Sean said, "I almost forgot—," and they shared a nervous laugh. "What did you forget?" she said.

He bit his lip before he said, "You know how I told you about a woman I couldn't stop thinking about?"

She nodded.

"Well, I can be a bit obsessive. Not in a bad way mind you," he quickly added, "just uh...well not in a good way either. So, in order to...uh think of something else I came up with a mission in case I ever saw her again."

Alana sent him a curious look. "A mission?"

"Yes." He lifted her hand before he reached into his jacket pocket and placed a handful of lipstick tubes in her palm. "You're right," he said with feeling. "These suckers are hard to find."

Alana stared down in awe at the tiny pile of discontinued lipsticks he'd been able to find. She counted five of them. "I can't believe you did this. This must have cost you a tiny fortune." She'd seen one tube online for two hundred dollars.

"I hope this can last you for a while."

"It will, thanks."

"Although I'm sure you don't need it."

She put the lipsticks in her handbag then took her used one out, looked at her reflection in the window (in a section where no one was seated) and applied it before smiling up at him. "I do because it's the best. The color's perfect, it leaves my lips moist, and it doesn't rub off."

"Even if you kiss someone?" Sean said in a low voice, his gaze heated.

"Yes," she said a little breathless. "Even then."

He lowered his head. "Mind if I find out?"

"No," Alana said, taking a step closer, "I don't mind at all."

His lips were as warm and sweet as a spiced bun right from the oven. He briefly drew away and whispered, "Now will you tell me?"

She blinked confused, still breathless from his kiss. "Tell you what?"

"Your name."

She stared at him surprised. "I haven't told you my name yet?"

Sean shook his head.

Alana smiled at him. A smile that wiped away all her yesterdays and welcomed the fresh scent of the present and the many tomorrows to come. "I'll tell you when we meet again. Same time, same place. Don't keep me waiting."

And for the rest of their lives, he never did.

ABOUT THE AUTHOR

Dara Girard, an award-winning, national bestselling author of more than fifty novels and many short stories, from romance to suspense, loves telling stories.

Born in the US to immigrant parents, Dara enjoys pulling from her Jamaican, British, Nigerian heritage and exposure to various cultures to bring what reviewers and fans call "vivid emotional stories" to life. She is best known for her popular Henson Series, the mysterious Clifton Sisters, and the fun Black Stockings Society.

Visit her website to sign up for her newsletter and get sneak peeks, monthly updates on new releases, and special offers.

For more information visit
www.daragirard.com